CATHERINE STOCK

ALEXANDER'S MIDNIGHT SNACK

A LITTLE ELEPHANT'S ABC

Clarion Books
TICKNOR & FIELDS : A HOUGHTON MIFFLIN COMPANY
New York

*For Jude, Jim,
and of course,
Alexander*

Clarion Books
Ticknor & Fields, a Houghton Mifflin Company
Text and Illustrations copyright © 1988 by Catherine Stock

Library of Congress Cataloging-in-Publication Data
Stock, Catherine.
Alexander's midnight snack:
A little elephant's ABC
Summary: A little elephant's midnight snack grows into
a feast composed of a different food for each letter of
the alphabet.
[1. Elephants—Fiction.   2. Food—Fiction.
3. Alphabet]   I. Title.
PZ7.S8635A1   1988   [E]   88-2608
ISBN 0-89919-512-1

Y 10 9 8 7 6 5 4 3 2 1

Alexander wakes up in the middle
of the night. He is thirsty.

His mother and father are fast
asleep, so he tiptoes down to the
kitchen to get a glass of water.

On the kitchen table is a piece of
Apple pie. Ahh, thinks Alexander.

Behind the pie is a **B**ox of raisin **B**uns.

And behind it he spies a tin of
Cinnamon Cookies. "Just one," says
Alexander to himself.

Then he spies a **D**ish of **D**oughnuts

and four (hopefully) hard-boiled
Eggs.

In the **F**ridge are some **F**ishcakes!
(Alexander *loves* **F**ishcakes.)

And some **G**ingersnaps. (Alexander
wonders what **G**ingersnaps are
doing in the fridge.)

Then he finds a pot of **H**oney,

a tub of chocolate chip Ice cream,

and a small Jar of raspberry Jam.

Watch out, Alexander! The **K**etchup! Oooops. Too late.

In the cupboard Alexander finds an orange. Oooo no…it's a *Lemon*!

Alexander tries to **Make** a
Milkshake. (What a **Mess**.)

Alexander sprinkles some **N**uts and
a cherry on his milkshake. Mmmm!
Good!

Next he sees an **O**range. **O**r is it a lemon? Alexander is worried.

He eats a **P**ickle instead.

Then Alexander finds a **Q**uarter of
a pound of Swiss cheese

and three slices of **R**oast beef.

I'll make a **S**andwich, thinks
Alexander,

a Toasted sandwich.

And afterward I'll have a piece of
pineapple **U**psidedown cake.

Then Alexander sees a jar of
pickled pigs trotters in **V**inegar.
(*Ugh!*)

"I don't feel **Well**," he groans. He quickly drinks his glass of **Water**.

This is what an **X**-ray of
Alexander's stomach looks like.

Then he **Y**awns

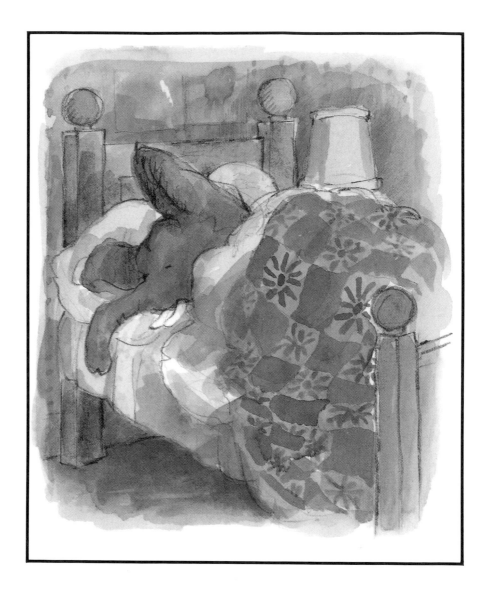

and stumbles off to bed.
ZZZZZZZZzzzzzzzzzzzzzzzzzz

And that may be the end of the alphabet, but it's not quite the end of Alexander's story. Because the next morning his mother comes down to the kitchen and this is what she sees…

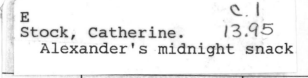